Blue Floats Away

words by Travis Jonker
pictures by Grant Snider

Abrams Books for Young Readers • New York

Little Blue lived near the North Pole with his parents.

They were close.

One day—*CRACK*—Blue was suddenly on his own, floating away.

Blue was surprised.
Blue's parents were surprised.

No one was prepared for this.

"I'll be back soon!"
Blue called as he floated away.

But he wasn't so sure.

Before long, Little Blue couldn't
see his parents anymore.
He couldn't see anything.

Except this.

He began to wonder if he would ever make it home again.

After days and days of nothing,
Blue began to see things.

New things.

Beautiful things.

He was so happy to have company.

Blue learned things from his new friends.
About wind and ocean currents.
Things that could help him get home.

Blue planned his return.

But something unplanned
was happening.

It was getting warmer,
and Little Blue was
getting smaller

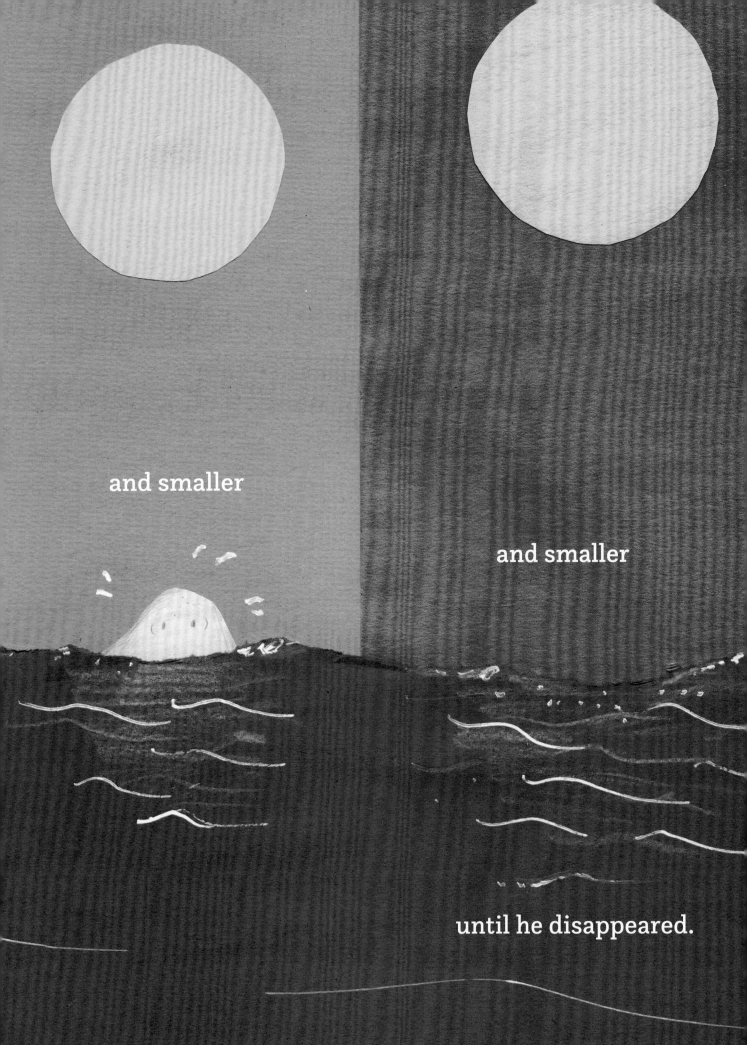

and smaller

and smaller

until he disappeared.

Blue's friends didn't know what to do.
So they went on their way.

But Blue wasn't gone.
He was changing.

Blue mixed with
the ocean water,
evaporated,
condensed,

and was transformed.

Soon, Blue began to see things.

New things.

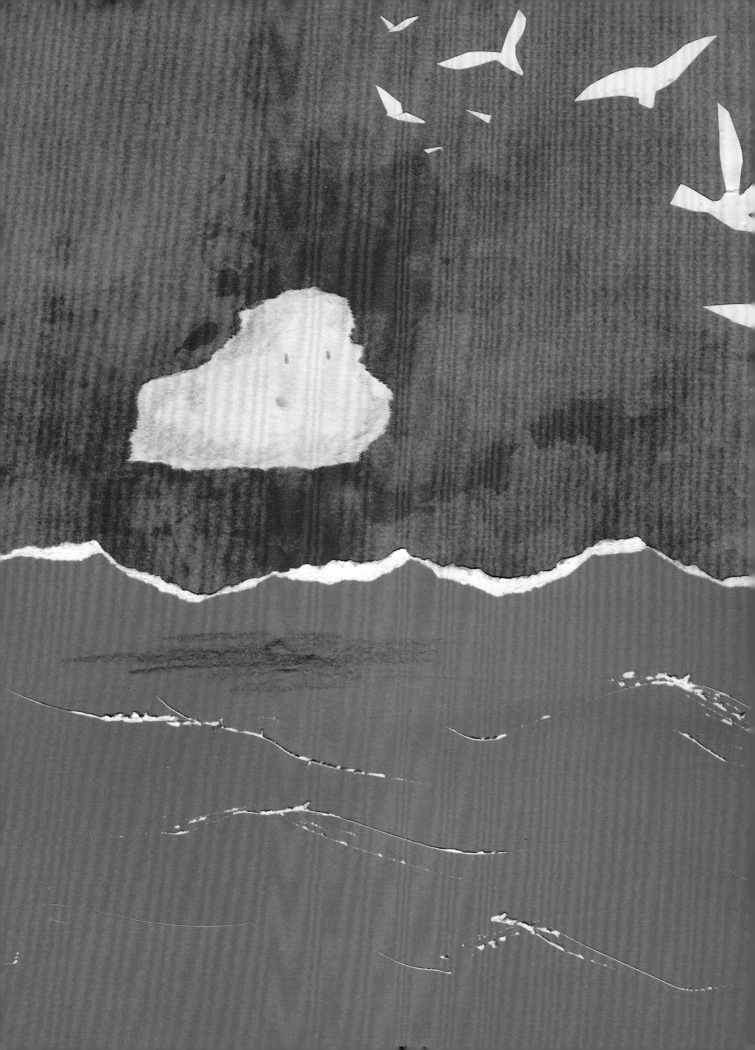

Beautiful things.

Blue learned things
from his new friends.

About the directions:
East, West, South...

and North.

Blue set a course for home.

On the way, he visited old friends.

It was getting colder,

and Little Blue was
getting bigger

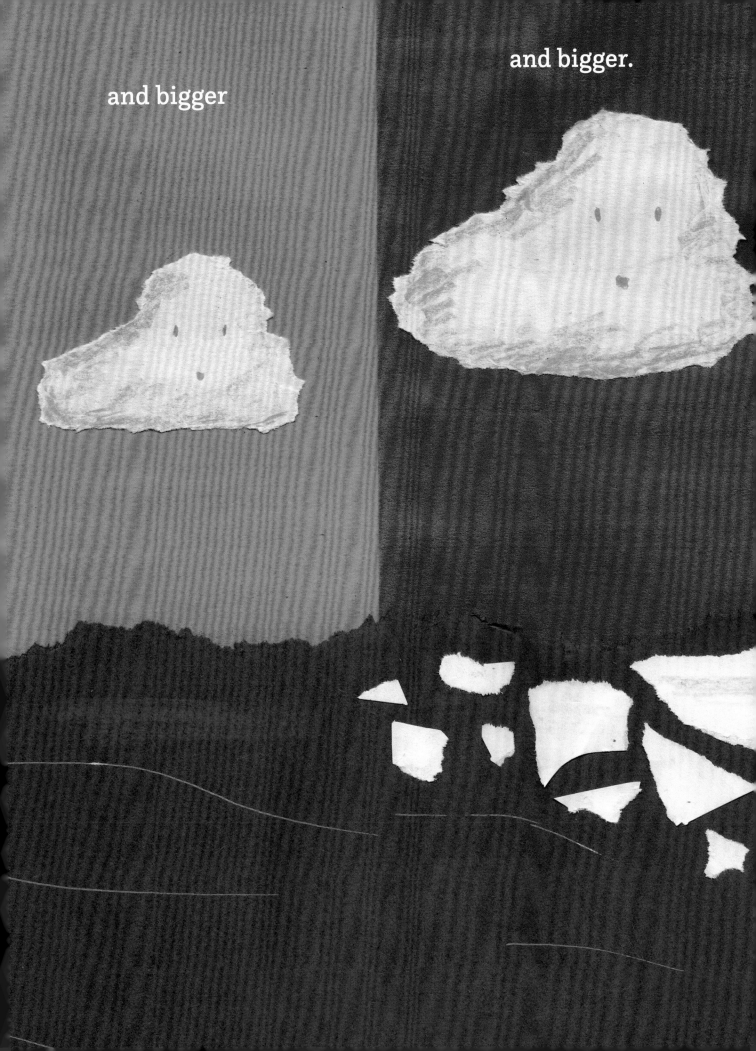

and bigger

and bigger.

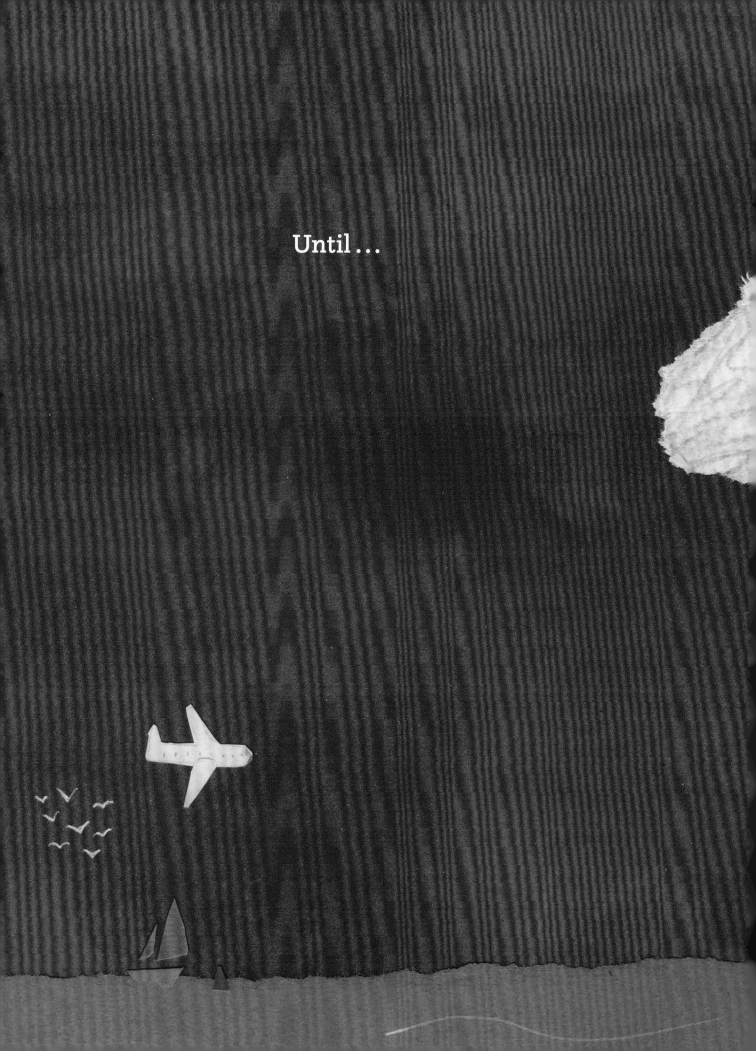

Until...

Little Blue saw his parents again.

Were *they* ever surprised.

Author's Note

Blue's story is also the story of the water cycle.

Blue begins as ice, melts into water, evaporates into gas, and condenses into precipitation in the form of snow.

The water cycle is happening all around our planet, with water changing from solid (ice) to liquid (water) to gas (water vapor) and back again. It makes life on Earth possible.

While Blue's story has a happy ending, polar ice is in real trouble. Temperatures on Earth have been rising due to human-created greenhouse gases. This is called climate change, and it's bad for our planet! Climate change causes ice at Earth's poles to melt and leads to more extreme weather—two things that make it more difficult for life on Earth.

Here are some things we can all do to help:

Use less energy. Turn off lights, and walk or ride a bike instead of using a car or truck.

Reduce, reuse, and recycle. By using less stuff and by reusing and recycling the stuff we already have, we can decrease greenhouse gases.

Take action! Volunteer with and donate money to groups fighting climate change. And write or call people who make laws and ask them to work on solving this problem.

By taking care of our planet, we can fight climate change and make the world a better place.

FOR COLINA
—T.J.

To Logan, for all your adventures
—G.S.

The illustrations for this book were made with cut paper, colored pencil, and white ink.

Library of Congress Cataloging-in-Publication Data:

Names: Jonker, Travis, author. | Snider, Grant, illustrator.
Title: Blue floats away / by Travis Jonker ; illustrated by Grant Snider.
Description: New York : Abrams Books for Young Readers, [2021] | Audience:
Ages 4 to 8. | Summary: Little Blue is very close to his iceberg parents
so when he suddenly breaks away from them, he promises to return and,
after traveling far and undergoing big changes, he may succeed.
Identifiers: LCCN 2020011961 | ISBN 9781419744235 (hardcover)
Subjects: CYAC: Icebergs—Fiction. | Change—Fiction. | Adventure and
adventurers—Fiction.
Classification: LCC PZ7.1.J76 Blu 2021 | DDC [E]—dc23
LC record available at https://lccn.loc.gov/2020011961

Text copyright © 2021 Travis Jonker
Illustrations copyright © 2021 Grant Snider
Book design by Pamela Notarantonio

Printed and bound in China
10 9 8 7 6 5 4 3 2 1

Abrams Books for Young Readers are available at special
discounts when purchased in quantity for premiums and promotions
as well as fundraising or educational use. Special editions
can also be created to specification. For details, contact
specialsales@abramsbooks.com or the address below.

ABRAMS The Art of Books
195 Broadway, New York, NY 10007
abramsbooks.com

MIX
Paper from
responsible sources
FSC
www.fsc.org   FSC® C144853